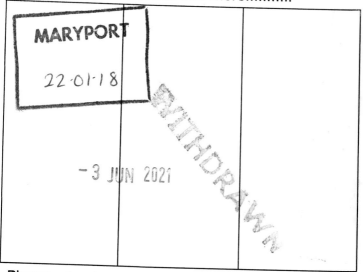
LONDON·SYDNEY

Franklin Watts
First published in Great Britain in 2017
by The Watts Publishing Group

Text © Steve Barlow and Steve Skidmore 2017
Illustrations © Andrew Tunney 2017
Cover design: Peter Scoulding
Executive Editor: Adrian Cole

ISBN 978 1 4451 5183 0
ebook ISBN 978 1 4451 5184 7
Library ebook ISBN 978 1 4451 5185 4

1 3 5 7 9 10 8 6 4 2

Printed in Great Britain

Franklin Watts
An imprint of
Hachette Children's Group
Part of The Watts Publishing Group
Carmelite House
50 Victoria Embankment
London EC4Y 0DZ

An Hachette UK Company
www.hachette.co.uk

www.franklinwatts.co.uk

How to be a Legend

Throughout the ages, great men and women have performed deeds so mighty that their names have passed into legend.

Could YOU be one of them?

In this book, you are Robin Hood, the hero of the adventure. You must make decisions that will affect how the adventure unfolds.

Each section of this book is numbered. At the end of most sections, you will have to make a choice. The choice you make will take you to a different section of the book.

Some of your choices will help you to complete the adventure successfully. But choose carefully, some of your decisions could be fatal!

If you fail, then start the adventure again, and learn from your mistake.

If you choose wisely, you will succeed!

Are you ready to be a hero? Have you got what it takes to become a legend?

You are Robin Hood. You live in Sherwood Forest with your band of outlaws including Little John, Friar Tuck, Will Scarlett and Maid Marian.

King Richard the Lionheart rules England, but has been captured whilst returning from the wars in the East. His brother, John, rules England in his place, helped by his evil supporters including the Sheriff of Nottingham and his deputy, Guy of Gisborne.

Your band of outlaws are sworn to fight injustice and defend the rights of ordinary people. To do this, you rob from the rich to give to the poor.

You have had information that a merchant is going to be passing through Sherwood Forest. He has a box of gold coins, collected by overcharging his customers and crooked dealing. You head into the heart of the forest to ambush him on your own ...

Go to section 1.

1

You are hiding in a ditch at the side of the track, waiting for the merchant to pass by.

You hear the sound of a horse and wagon rattling down the road. You look up to see two armed guards riding in front of the merchant's

wagon. The merchant sits on the front of the
wagon, guiding his horse.

**If you wish to attack the merchant and his
guards, go to 45.**

**If you want to sneak onto the wagon, go
to 16.**

2

You step into the middle of the road and motion the wagon to stop. The other outlaws surround the wagon.

"We will not hurt you, but we need your wagon," you say.

"But this is all I have," replies the man.

"I am sorry," you reply, "but someone's life is at stake." You send the man on his way.

You take the wagon and ride towards Nottingham. As you approach the gatehouse you hide your weapons, and disguise yourselves using old cloaks to cover your clothing.

Go to 37.

3

"We must rescue Marian!" you cry. "We'll set out for Nottingham immediately!"

Little John holds up a hand. "Peace, Robin. We must consider what is best to do. We cannot go into Nottingham without more knowledge and without making a plan. We would stand no chance against the sheriff's and Gisborne's men."

You realise that he is right, you are allowing your emotions to cloud your judgement.

Go to 23.

4

You make your way through hidden forest tracks, avoiding any of Gisborne's men that might be lying in wait for you ...

Eventually, you reach the edge of the forest to see the city of Nottingham with its great castle ahead of you. The entrance to the city is heavily guarded by the sheriff's men.

If you asked for Tuck's help, go to 40.
If you didn't, go to 33.

5

Many hours later you wake up to find yourself chained to a wall in a dark, damp prison. You know you will never escape from here. Rats scurry around the dirty floor. They will be your only companions until the day you die ...

You'll never become a legend locked in a damp cell!

To begin again, go to 1.

6

"You're coming with us," you say. "Order your men not to attack us."

You push the sheriff from the balcony. Little John catches him.

You too leap down to join Marian and the outlaws. With your sword prodding the sheriff's back, you walk through the crowds and the unarmed guards. They part to let you through.

However, as you get to the gatehouse a young soldier rushes at you, sword drawn. You parry his attack and knock him to the floor.

"He should pay for that with his life," says Little John.

"No!" says Marian. "Be merciful, Robin.
Let him go."

To do what Little John says, go to 21.
If you would rather follow Marian's advice,
go to 39.

7

"Head into the trees and hide," you cry. The outlaws obey you and run for cover.

Gisborne's men give chase, shooting arrows and crossbow bolts.

You see Will Scarlett crash to the ground, wounded. You hurry towards him, but as you do you feel an arrow pierce your side. Dropping down injured, you look up and see Gisborne's men moving towards you. Their swords are raised. You know there is no escape for you ...

With that sort of cowardly behaviour, you'll never be a legend!

Go back to 1 and begin again.

8

You realise that you cannot win this fight, so you leap into the bushes, avoiding the crossbow bolts that the guards shoot at you.

You speed through the forest tracks until you are safe.

You know that you have missed out on a rich haul and should have asked the other outlaws to help you ambush the merchant. You tell yourself not to be so hasty again as you head deep into the greenwood to your camp.

Go to 30.

9

You think quickly. "Apples and vegetables for the sheriff's store," you reply.

A guard climbs onto the wagon and opens a barrel. "It's full of salted meat!" he says.

"Arrest these men!" orders the captain.

"To arms!" you cry. You leap from the wagon to give battle with the other outlaws, but as you do so, you are clubbed to the ground by one of the guards. You pass into unconsciousness.

Go to 5.

10

"I would rather die a free man!" you say.

"Then I am happy to help you fulfil your wish," your enemy replies. "Loose!"

You cry out as a volley of arrows strikes you.

You're free, but dead! That won't help Marian.

To begin again, go to 1.

11

You creep towards the front of the wagon and peer through the covered opening. The merchant is sitting on the box seat and guiding his horse.

You pick up a wooden club that is lying in a corner and in one movement knock the merchant unconscious. You haul him inside the wagon.

The guards continue to ride ahead of the wagon, unaware of your presence.

If you want to shoot the guards, go to 45.

If you decide to force them off their horses, go to 27.

12

You pull your hidden bow from your cloak, nock an arrow, aim and shoot the hangman.

Immediately, the guards on the ramparts shoot crossbow bolts into the courtyard. People scream and run as the crowd dash for cover.

Taking advantage of the situation, you and the outlaws fight your way through the guards surrounding the scaffold. You manage to fell several of the sheriff's men, but you are outnumbered. Will Scarlett, Little John and Friar

Tuck all fall beneath the guards' deadly swords.

Fighting desperately, you manage to make your way up the wooden steps. "Marian!" you cry.

She looks and gives a warning, "To your left!"

You spin around, but are too slow. You see a flash of steel and your body is racked with pain as the guard's blade cuts into your side.

Your last sight is that of Marian staring at you in horror.

So near, but so far!

Go back to 1 and try again.

13

You draw your sword and charge out of the trees towards the village. The other outlaws follow you, arrows nocked and bows drawn.

Gisborne's men meet your attack head on and begin to fight back. The fighting is fierce as you and the outlaws engage with the enemy.

Just as it seems that you are winning the battle, more armed soldiers appear from out of the trees. You are outnumbered!

To flee into the forest, go to 7.
To continue the fight, go to 46.

14

You know that Friar Tuck will be needed, so you turn to Much, the miller's son. "Go to Tuck's friary and tell him what has happened," you say. "We will meet you both in Nottingham and he can tell us how to get into the castle through the tunnels."

Much hurries off, while you and the other outlaws prepare to head to Nottingham.

Go to 47.

15

"I agree with Little John," you say.

You head back into the forest to wait for a merchant to pass by. Eventually, a wagon driven by an old man and full of wooden barrels trundles down the road towards you.

If you wish to steal the wagon, go to 2.
If you wish to offer to buy the wagon, go to 48.

16

You wait until the guards have ridden by and the wagon is level with you. Carefully, you climb up from the ditch and jump onto the back of the wagon, without being heard.

Taking your knife, you cut into the cloth covering the wagon and step inside. You see several barrels and wooden chests.

If you wish to check what is inside the barrels, go to 41.

To open a wooden chest, go to 49.

17

"We head to the castle to rescue her now!" you say.

You lead the outlaws through Nottingham's crowded narrow streets. You soon reach the castle gatehouse but it is guarded by a troop of heavily armed men.

"What do you men want?" asks the captain of the guard.

"We have news for the sheriff regarding the outlaw, Robin Hood," you reply.

"Very well, pass."

That was easy, you think as the portcullis is pulled up and you walk into the inner court. You stop, waiting for a second gate to be opened.

At that moment, the portcullis slams down behind you, trapping you and your men.

"The sheriff was expecting you!" laughs the captain. You are all helpless as the guards aim crossbows through the portcullis.

"Shoot!" he orders. It is the last thing you hear as you succumb to the deadly missiles.

Thinking you could just walk into the castle is only legendary for its stupidity!

Go to 1 and begin again.

18

"We don't have time to help the villagers," you say. The other outlaws look disappointed, and reluctantly agree to carry on towards Nottingham.

However, you are only a few hundred metres from the village, when another troop of Gisborne's men appear from the trees. They see you and charge at you, weapons drawn.

If you wish to fight Gisborne's men, go to 32.

If you want to avoid the fight, go to 7.

19

"Tuck knows the secret ways into the city," you say. "We will wait for him."

Eventually, your patience is rewarded, as within the hour Much the miller's son arrives with Friar Tuck. You explain the situation to him quickly.

"We will use the tunnels to get into the city," says Tuck. "Follow me ..."

Go to 42.

20

You leap towards the merchant with your knife drawn, but at that moment the wagon hits a rut in the track, and you're knocked off balance. The merchant lets loose the crossbow bolt, which hits you in the chest. You cry out in pain and crash to the wooden floor. You are helpless as the guards leap into the wagon, their deadly swords raised. Thankfully, your agony is short-lived as you pass into blackness.

Your adventure has ended almost before it has begun!

Start again at 1.

21

You nod agreement and move towards the soldier, sword drawn.

At that moment, the soldier reaches into his tunic and pulls out a hidden dagger. Before you can react he leaps at you, the metal glinting in the light.

Your cry of pain lasts no more than a second as death envelops you.

Only honourable people become legends!

Go back to 1 and start again.

22

There is a cry from the crowd as a troop of guards move out of the castle with Marian. Her hands are manacled. One of the sheriff's men drags her through the assembled citizens and up the scaffold's wooden steps. A hooded hangman waits for her.

"You will pay for this," you mutter.

At that moment the sheriff and Guy of Gisborne appear at the castle balcony. The crowd are quietened.

"People of Nottingham," announces the

sheriff. "This is what happens to those who disobey the law!" He signals to the hangman. "Do your duty!"

If you wish to rush at the scaffold to rescue Marian, go to 12.

If you wish to try to get onto the balcony, go to 44.

23

"How was Marian captured?" you ask Alan.

"She was lured into a trap by a false messenger," he replies. "He told Marian her old nurse was ill. She went home to visit the old woman, but Gisborne's men were lying in wait. They have taken her to Nottingham castle, where the sheriff has announced that she is to stand trial."

"Then we will have to get into the castle," you decide.

"Friar Tuck knows of the secret tunnels that lead into the castle," says Will. "But he has retired to his friary, do we have the time to call on his help?"

If you want Tuck's help, go to 14.

If you don't think you have time to call on his help, go to 47.

24

You draw your sword and parry the first guard's attack. You force your opponent backwards, with your superior sword-fighting skills. He stumbles over a tree trunk and you leap in for the kill.

However, at that moment, you hear a cry.

"Drop your sword, outlaw!"

You turn to see the other guard pointing a loaded crossbow at you.

If you wish to surrender, go to 38.

To flee into the forest, go to 8.

25

You order the outlaws to nock their bows and take aim.

At your command the air is filled with a volley of deadly arrows. Gisborne's men drop to the ground. The ones who survive look around in confusion, wondering where this attack has come from.

Another volley takes out more of Gisborne's men and soon there are only two left. They drop their weapons and hold up their hands in surrender.

The villagers give you heartfelt cheers as you move into the village.

Little John points at the two surviving soldiers. "We can't let them go," he says. "They will tell the sheriff where we are. We should put them to the sword."

If you want to take Little John's advice, and approach a soldier, go to 21.

If you wish to question the soldiers, go to 29.

"Salted meat for the sheriff's store," you reply.

A guard climbs onto the wagon and opens a barrel. "He's right!" he says.

"Pass on," the guard tells you.

You head through the gates into Nottingham. You make your way to a tavern where you know there is a friendly innkeeper and his wife. They have helped you before in your fight against the sheriff.

You enter the tavern and are amazed to see Friar Tuck. "I heard the news about Marian and made my way here," he tells you. "She has been found guilty of being an outlaw. She is to be executed in the castle courtyard tomorrow morning!"

If you wish to try to rescue Marian immediately, go to 17.

If you wish to wait until tomorrow, go to 35.

27

With a flick of the reins, you urge the horse forward at pace.

As you hurtle down the track, the guards turn around, but they are too slow. The wagon crashes into them, causing their horses to rear up and sending the guards tumbling onto the hard forest track. Their horses bolt away, leaving the guards cursing as you gallop out of sight with your captured haul!

You laugh and head towards your camp, deep in the greenwood.

Go to 43.

28

"Let's try to get across the moat," you tell the others.

You and the other outlaws head to the east of the city, to the area that Will had spotted as a way in.

You wade into the cold water and begin to swim across the moat. You are halfway across when there is a cry from the city walls — you've been spotted!

"Retreat!" you order as the guards open fire. Crossbow bolts rain down on you, hitting several of the outlaws. You manage to make your way back to the bank, but as you haul yourself out a bolt hits you in the back. You fall back into the water, which begins to turn red around you.

That choice didn't go swimmingly!

Go back to 1 and begin again.

29

You shake your head. "No, these men could be useful to us."

You stand over the terrified soldiers. "What do you know of Gisborne's plans?" you ask.

"Gisborne has sent troops into the forest to search for you," croaks one. "He thought you would come out of your lair to try to rescue Marian. He hopes to ambush you …"

"Then we will avoid his men by taking the back roads into Nottingham." You turn to one of the villagers. "Tie these men up and we will deal with them on our return …"

Go to 4.

30

You arrive back at your camp, where you tell Little John and Will Scarlett about your failed attempt to ambush the merchant.

"The poor people of Nottingham would have been well served with that money," says Little John. "Couldn't Marian have helped you to ambush the merchant?"

You look puzzled. "She wasn't with me. Is she not here?"

Will Scarlett shakes his head. "We thought she was with you."

At that moment Alan-a-Dale runs into the camp, breathless. "Marian has been captured by

Guy of Gisborne," he cries out. "She has been taken to Nottingham castle!"

If you want to head to Nottingham immediately, go to 3.

If you want to make a plan, go to 23.

31

"You will have what you deserve," you say and plunge your sword into his body.

But with the sheriff dead, there is no reason for the guards to lay down their weapons. They pick them up and charge towards the outlaws.

You leap from the balcony to help your men, but as you do a crossbow bolt pierces your side and you drop to the ground, dead.

It's no good fighting like a legend if you're thinking like a numbskull!

Go back to 1.

32

"Defend yourselves," you shout. Your men begin to let loose with their arrows, taking out several of Gisborne's soldiers.

However, the others regroup and charge

towards you. You and the outlaws fight for your lives, cutting down several of your enemies.

Although you are winning, the noise from the battle alerts the soldiers that were attacking the village, and they soon appear.

Desperately you fight on, but soon you are surrounded. Little John and Will Scarlett fall to the ground, hit by crossbow bolts and eventually you are the only outlaw left standing ...

The captain calls out, "Surrender, outlaw, or join your friends!"

If you wish to do as he says, go to 38.
If you wish to continue the fight, go to 10.

33

You send Little John and Will Scarlett to see if they can find a way to get into the city undetected.

After an anxious wait, they finally return and deliver their findings.

"We can head to the east of the city, swim across the moat and climb up the walls," suggests Will. "I couldn't see any guards there."

"There are many merchants heading into the

city," says Little John. "I think we should hijack a wagon and go through the gates in disguise."

If you wish to follow Little John's plan, go to 15.

If you wish to follow Will Scarlett's plan, go to 28.

34

You close the wooden chest and push it towards the back.

Suddenly, the wagon jolts causing the chest to fall and crash onto the forest track.

There are loud cries as the wagon comes to a sudden stop. You leap from the wagon to see the guards charging towards you.

If you wish to fight your way out, go to 24.

If you wish to surrender, go to 38.

If you decide to head into the forest, go to 8.

35

"We won't be able to get into the castle dungeons to rescue Marian," you say. "We will have to wait until she is brought out into the open."

You rest for the night at the tavern, before rising early and setting off to the castle courtyard. You lead the outlaws through Nottingham's crowded narrow streets, joining a throng of people who are also making their way towards the castle.

Blending in with these citizens, you safely pass by the gatehouse guards into the castle courtyard. In the centre is a wooden scaffold which has been prepared for Marian. Guards line the castle ramparts, crossbows at the ready to deal with anyone who might try to stop Marian's fate. You order the other outlaws to spread out amongst the crowd and wait for a signal.

Go to 22.

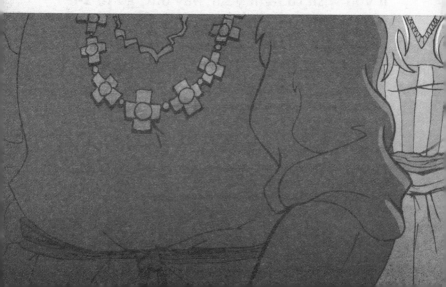

"We have to help the villagers," you tell the others.

By the time you reach the scene of the fighting, all is quiet. The men and women of the village are kneeling on the ground.

The captain of Gisborne's men stands over an elderly woman.

"We know there is a band of outlaws in the forest," you hear him shout. "Where is this fellow, Robin Hood? Tell me or suffer the consequences!"

"He's closer than you think," you mutter.

If you wish to charge at the enemy, go to 13.

If you wish to use your bows and arrows to attack, go to 25.

37

The city guards stop the wagon and eye you and the outlaws suspiciously.

"What is in the barrels?" asks the guard captain.

If the old man told you what is in the barrels, go to 26.

If he didn't, go to 9.

38

You drop your weapon and raise your hands.

Your enemy steps forward and smashes your head with the butt of his crossbow. You drop to the floor, unconscious.

Go to 5.

39

"Think yourself lucky, boy," you tell the soldier. "Robin Hood is not a cold-hearted killer."

Using the sheriff as a hostage, you and the outlaws reach the main gatehouse. You order the guards to bring you horses, and soon you and the outlaws are speeding into the greenwood.

Go to 50.

"We will wait for Tuck to join us," you tell the others. "But we need to find a way to get into the city undetected, in case he doesn't arrive in time."

You send Little John and Will Scarlett on a scouting mission.

Sometime later they return and deliver their findings.

"We can head to the east of the city, swim across the moat and climb up the walls," suggests Will. "I couldn't see any guards there."

"There are many merchants heading into the city," says Little John, "I think we should hijack a wagon and go through the gates in disguise."

You know that time is running out to rescue Marian.

If you wish to follow Little John's plan, go to 15.

If you wish to follow Will Scarlett's plan, go to 28.

If you wish to wait and see if Tuck arrives, go to 19.

41

You prise open the lid of one of the barrels and let out a cry of disgust — the barrel is full of rotting fish!

The wagon comes to a sudden halt. "Who's there?" cries the merchant. You have given yourself away!

The cloth opening is thrust open as the merchant aims a loaded crossbow at you. "Surrender, thief!" he cries. Behind him you see the two guards heading towards the wagon.

If you wish to leap from the wagon, go to 8.

If you wish to fight your way out, go to 20.

If you wish to surrender, go to 38.

42

Tuck leads you back into the forest and shows you a hidden cave.

"This way," he says, lighting a torch. He leads you and the outlaws through a series of dark, dank tunnels.

Eventually, you reach a set of stone steps. "This leads to the cellar of a tavern. The

innkeeper is no friend of the sheriff and will be glad to help us."

Soon you and the outlaws are in the tavern, where the landlord tells you the latest news of Marian.

"She has been found guilty of being an outlaw, and is to be executed in the castle courtyard tomorrow morning," he tells you.

If you wish to try to rescue Marian immediately, go to 17.

If you wish to wait until tomorrow, go to 35.

43

You arrive back at the camp, where Will Scarlett and Little John marvel at your tale of how you robbed the merchant.

You open up the chests full of silver coins. "The poor people of Nottingham will be thankful for this money," laughs Will. "Maid Marian can begin to distribute it."

"Where is Marian?" you ask.

Little John looks puzzled. "We thought she was with you."

At that moment Alan-a-Dale runs into the camp, breathless. "Marian has been captured by Guy of Gisborne," he cries out. "She has been taken to Nottingham castle!"

If you want to head to Nottingham immediately, go to 3.

If you want to make a plan, go to 23.

44

You beckon Little John towards you and explain your plan. He moves through the crowd, stands in front of the balcony and cups his hands in front of his body.

The sheriff is still speaking as you run at Little John and leap forwards. He catches your foot and throws you into the air.

Spinning like an acrobat, you land on the balcony and, before he can react, throw Gisborne from it. As he lies stunned on the ground, you hold your sword to the sheriff's throat.

"Tell your men to lay down their weapons," you tell him, "or suffer the consequences."

The sheriff is terrified. "Do as he says," he orders. His men obey him.

"Release Marian," you say.

Friar Tuck moves to the scaffold and frees Marian from her manacles. She and the outlaws move through the crowd towards the gatehouse.

"What are you going to do with me?" asks the sheriff.

If you wish to kill the sheriff, go to 31.

If you wish to take him with you, go to 6.

45

You string your bow, take aim at the first guard and let fly. The arrow hits the guard in the body, but he doesn't fall to the ground. You realise he is wearing armour under his tunic!

The guards charge towards you. You shoot another arrow, but again the missile just bounces off the armour. The guards leap from their horses.

If you wish to continue the fight, go to 24.

If you wish to retreat into the forest, go to 8.

46

"Fight for your lives!" you cry out. The outlaws respond to your command and redouble their efforts. The air is filled with arrows and crossbow bolts.

One of Gisborne's men closes in on Will Scarlett, sword raised. You quickly nock your arrow, draw back your bow and let fly. The soldier drops to the floor and Will nods a grateful thanks.

Slowly, your men take control of the fight, and soon there are just a couple of Gisborne's men left standing. They drop their weapons and hold up their hands in surrender.

Little John looks at you. "We can't let them go," he says. "They will tell the sheriff where we are. We should put them to the sword."

If you want to take Little John's advice, and approach a solider, go to 21.

If you wish to question the soldiers, go to 29.

47

You gather your weapons and set off for Nottingham. Your journey takes you down forest paths known only to you and your band of outlaws.

You are nearing a small village, when you see plumes of smoke billowing into the air. You hear cries of distress and fighting, so you send Will Scarlett to investigate.

A few minutes later he reports back. "There's a band of soldiers dressed in the uniform of Guy of Gisborne," he tells you. "They're burning the houses and seizing goods. What should we do?"

If you wish to carry on to Nottingham, go to 18.

If you wish to help the villagers, go to 36.

48

You step out into the road, causing the wagon to come to a halt.

"What do you want of me?" asks the terrified merchant.

"We need your wagon and goods," you say. "We will buy them for a fair price." You hold out a bag of silver coins. The man immediately agrees.

"What is in the barrels?" you ask.

"Salted meat for the sheriff's storerooms," he replies.

You hand over the money, take the wagon and with Little John drive towards the city gatehouse. As you approach, you put on old cloaks to disguise yourselves. The other outlaws walk behind the wagon, weapons hidden from view.

Go to 37.

49

You carefully prise open the wooden chest to reveal hundreds of silver coins.

You open another chest and reveal even more! This would be a mighty haul indeed! However, you know that you won't be able to carry more than one chest, and wonder what to do.

If you want to take just one chest, go to 34.

If you wish to try to capture the wagon, go to 11.

50

You don't want the sheriff to know where your hideout is, so you tie him onto a mule, facing backwards, and send him off back to Nottingham.

Back in your camp, you celebrate Marian's rescue, and your victory over Gisborne and the sheriff, with a mighty feast.

Alan-a-Dale sings a song about your latest feat. All the outlaws agree that you will go down in history for your struggle against injustice and tyranny. You are a legend!

BEOWULF

STEVE BARLOW · STEVE SKIDMORE

ART BY ANDREW TUNNEY

You are Beowulf, heroic warrior of the Geats, a bold and warlike Scandinavian people.

You have already helped your neighbour, the King of Denmark, by destroying Grendel. This monster had killed many of the King's most loyal men, but you fought and defeated it with your bare hands.

You hoped the threat was over, but the very next night, Grendel's mother appeared and killed even more men.

You tracked the monster to its lair beneath a lake and, following a ferocious battle, cut off her head.

Since those dark but triumphant days, you have become king of your people. But now a new threat has emerged — a threat that it will take all your skill and courage to overcome ...

Continue the adventure in:

¡HERO LEGENDS
BEOWULF

About the 2Steves

"The 2Steves" are
Britain's most popular
writing double act
for young people,
specialising in comedy
and adventure. They
perform regularly in schools and libraries,
and at festivals, taking the power of words
and story to audiences of all ages.

Together they have written many books,
including the *I HERO Immortals* and *iHorror* series.

About the illustrator:
Andrew Tunney (aka 2hands)

Andrew is a freelance artist and writer based in
Manchester, UK. He has worked in illustration, character
design, comics, print, clothing and live-art. His work
has been featured by Comics Alliance, ArtSlant Street,
DigitMag, The Bluecoat, Starburst and Forbidden Planet.
He earned the nickname "2hands" because he can draw
with both hands at once. He is not ambidextrous; he just
works hard.

Have you completed the I HERO Quests?

Battle to save an underwater world in Atlantis Quest:

MENACE FROM THE DEEP
Steve Barlow – Steve Skidmore

978 1 4451 2867 2 pb
978 1 4451 2867 9 ebook

OCEAN ALLIANCE
Steve Barlow – Steve Skidmore

978 1 4451 2870 2 pb
978 1 4451 2871 9 ebook

BATTLE FOR THE SEAS
Steve Barlow – Steve Skidmore

978 1 4451 2876 4 pb
978 1 4451 2877 1 ebook

ATLANTIS ASSAULT
Steve Barlow – Steve Skidmore

978 1 4451 2873 3 pb
978 1 4451 2874 0 ebook

Defeat the Red Queen in Blood Crown Quest:

SANDS OF BLOOD
Steve Barlow – Steve Skidmore

978 1 4451 1499 6 pb
978 1 4451 1503 0 ebook

DRAGON MOUNTAIN
Steve Barlow – Steve Skidmore

978 1 4451 1500 9 pb
978 1 4451 1504 7 ebook

DEMON SEA
Steve Barlow – Steve Skidmore

978 1 4451 1501 6 pb
978 1 4451 1505 4 ebook

CITY OF THE DEAD
Steve Barlow – Steve Skidmore

978 1 4451 1502 3 pb
978 1 4451 1506 1 ebook

Also by the 2Steves…

978 1 4451 4081 0 pb
978 1 4451 4082 7 eBook

Immortals

HERO

Dragon

Steve Barlow – Steve Skidmore

You are the last Dragon Warrior.
A dark, evil force stirs within the
Iron Mines. Grull the Cruel's
army is on the march! YOU must
stop Grull.

978 1 4451 4088 9 pb
978 1 4451 4087 2 eBook

Immortals

HERO

Mermaid

Steve Barlow – Steve Skidmore

You are a noble mermaid –
your father is King Edmar.
The Tritons are attacking your home
of Coral City. YOU must save the Merrow
people by finding the Lady of the Sea.

978 1 4451 4084 1 pb
978 1 4451 4085 8 eBook

Immortals

HERO

Superhero

Steve Barlow – Steve Skidmore

You are Olympian, a superhero.
Your enemy, Doctor Robotic,
is turning people into mind slaves.
Now YOU must put a stop to his
plans before it's too late!

978 1 4451 3958 6 pb
978 1 4451 3961 6 eBook

Immortals

HERO

Wizard

Steve Barlow – Steve Skidmore

You are a young wizard.
The evil Witch Queen has captured
Prince Bron. Now YOU must rescue
him before she takes control of
Nine Mountain kingdom!